Through Grandpa's Eyes

Patricia MacLachlan   *Pictures by* Deborah Kogan Ray

 HarperCollins*Publishers*

Through Grandpa's Eyes
Text copyright © 1980 by Patricia MacLachlan
Illustrations copyright © 1980 by Deborah Ray
Manufactured in China. For information address HarperCollins
Children's Books, a division of HarperCollins Publishers,
10 East 53rd Street, New York, NY 10022.

Library of Congress Cataloging-in-Publication Data
MacLachlan, Patricia.
    Through Grandpa's Eyes.
    Summary: A young boy learns a different way of
seeing the world from his blind grandfather.
    [1. Blind—Fiction.   2. Grandfathers—Fiction]
I. Ray, Deborah.   II. Title.
PZ7.M2225Th   [Fic]   79-2019
ISBN 0-06-024044-X. —ISBN 0-06-024043-1 (lib. bdg.)
ISBN 0-06-443041-3 (pbk.)

13 14 15 SCP 25 24 23 22

Of all the houses that I know, I like my grandpa's best. My friend Peter has a new glass house with pebble-path gardens that go nowhere. And Maggie lives next door in an old wooden house with rooms behind rooms, all with carved doors and brass doorknobs. They are fine houses. But Grandpa's house is my favorite. Because I see it through Grandpa's eyes.

Grandpa is blind. He doesn't see the house the way I do. He has his own way of seeing.

In the morning, the sun pushes through the curtains into my eyes. I burrow down into the covers to get away, but the light follows me. I give up, throw back the covers, and run to Grandpa's room.

The sun wakes Grandpa differently from the way it wakes me. He says it touches him, *warming* him awake. When I peek around the door, Grandpa is already up and doing his morning exercises. Bending and stretching by the bed. He stops and smiles because he hears me.

"Good morning, John."

"Where's Nana?" I ask him.

"Don't you know?" he says, bending and stretching. "Close your eyes, John, and look through my eyes."

I close my eyes. Down below, I hear the banging of pots and the sound of water running that I didn't hear before.

"Nana is in the kitchen, making breakfast," I say.

When I open my eyes again, I can see Grandpa nodding at me. He is tall with dark gray hair. And his eyes are sharp blue even though they are not sharp seeing.

I exercise with Grandpa. Up and down. Then I try to exercise with my eyes closed.

"One, two," says Grandpa, "three, four."

"Wait!" I cry. I am still on one, two when Grandpa is on three, four.

I fall sideways. Three times. Grandpa laughs as he hears my thumps on the carpet.

"Breakfast!" calls Nana from downstairs.

"I smell eggs frying," says Grandpa. He bends his head close to mine. "And buttered toast."

The wooden banister on the stairway has been worn smooth from Grandpa running his fingers up and down. I walk behind him, my fingers following Grandpa's smooth path.

We go into the kitchen.

"I smell flowers," says Grandpa.

"What flowers?" I ask.

He smiles. He loves guessing games.

"Not violets, John, not peonies…"

"Carnations!" I cry. *I* love guessing games.

"Silly." Grandpa laughs. "Marigolds. Right, Nana?"

Nana laughs, too.

"That's too easy," she says, putting two plates of food in front of us.

"It's not too easy," I protest. "How can Grandpa tell? All the smells mix together in the air."

"Close your eyes, John," says Nana. "Tell me what breakfast is."

"I smell the eggs. I smell the toast," I say, my eyes closed. "And something else. The something else doesn't smell good."

"*That* something else," says Nana, smiling, "is the marigolds."

When he eats, Grandpa's plate of food is a clock.

"Two eggs at nine o'clock and toast at two o'clock," says Nana to Grandpa. "And a dollop of jam."

"A dollop of jam," I tell Grandpa, "at six o'clock."

I make my plate of food a clock, too, and eat through Grandpa's eyes.

After breakfast, I follow Grandpa's path through the dining room to the living room, to the window that he opens to feel the weather outside, to the table where he finds his pipe, and to his cello in the corner.

"Will you play with me, John?" he asks.

He tunes our cellos without looking. I play with a music stand and music before me. I know all about sharps and flats. I see them on the music. But Grandpa plays them. They are in his fingers. For a moment I close my eyes and play through Grandpa's eyes. My fingering hand slides up and down the cello neck— toward the pegs for flats, toward the bridge for sharps. But with my eyes closed my bow falls from the strings.

"Listen," says Grandpa. "I'll play a piece I learned when I was your age. It was my favorite."

He plays the tune while I listen. That is the way Grandpa learns new pieces. By listening.

"Now," says Grandpa. "Let's do it together."

"That's fine," says Grandpa as we play. "But C sharp, John," he calls to me. "C sharp!"

Later, Nana brings out her clay to sculpt my Grandpa's head.

"Sit still," she grumbles.

"I won't," he says, imitating her grumbly voice, making us laugh.

While she works, Grandpa takes out his piece of wood. He holds it when he's thinking. His fingers move back and forth across the wood, making smooth paths like the ones on the stair banister.

"Can I have a piece of thinking wood, too?" I ask.

Grandpa reaches in his shirt pocket and tosses a small bit of wood in my direction. I catch it. It is smooth with no splinters.

"The river is up," says Nana.

Grandpa nods a short nod. "It rained again last night. Did you hear the gurgling in the rain gutter?"

As they talk, my fingers begin a river on my thinking wood. The wood will winter in my pocket so when I am not at Grandpa's house I can still think about Nana, Grandpa, and the river.

When Nana is finished working, Grandpa runs his hand over the sculpture, his fingers soft and quick like butterflies.

"It looks like me," he says, surprised.

My eyes have already told me that it looks like Grandpa. But he shows me how to feel his face with my three middle fingers, and then the clay face.

"Pretend your fingers are water," he tells me.

My waterfall fingers flow down his clay head, filling in the spaces beneath the eyes like little pools before they flow down over the cheeks. It does feel like Grandpa. This time my fingers tell me.

Grandpa and I walk outside, through the front yard and across the field to the river. Grandpa has not been blind forever. He remembers in his mind the gleam of the sun on the river, the Queen Anne's lace in the meadow, and every dahlia in his garden. But he gently takes my elbow as we walk so that I can help show him the path.

"I feel a south wind," says Grandpa.

I can tell which way the wind is blowing because I see the way the tops of the trees lean. Grandpa tells by the feel of the meadow grasses and by the way his hair blows against his face.

When we come to the riverbank, I see that Nana was right. The water is high and has cut in by the willow tree. It flows around and among the roots of the tree, making paths. Paths like Grandpa's on the stair banister and on the thinking wood. I see a blackbird with a red patch on its wing sitting on a cattail. Without thinking, I point my finger.

"What is that bird, Grandpa?" I ask excitedly.

"*Conk-a-ree,*" the bird calls to us.

"A red-winged blackbird," says Grandpa promptly.

He can't see my finger pointing. But he hears the song of the bird.

"And somewhere behind the blackbird," he says, listening, "a song sparrow."

I hear a scratchy song, and I look and look until I see the earth-colored bird that Grandpa knows is here.

Nana calls from the front porch of the house.

"Nana's made hot bread for lunch," he tells me happily. "And spice tea." Spice tea is his favorite.

I close my eyes, but all I can smell is the wet earth by the river.

As we walk back to the house, Grandpa stops suddenly. He bends his head to one side, listening. He points his finger upward.

"Honkers," he whispers.

I look up and see a flock of geese, high in the clouds, flying in a V.

"Canada geese," I tell him.

"Honkers," he insists. And we both laugh.

We walk up the path again and to the yard where Nana is painting the porch chairs. Grandpa smells the paint.

"What color, Nana?" he asks. "I cannot smell the color."

"Blue," I tell him, smiling. "Blue like the sky."

"Blue like the color of Grandpa's eyes," Nana says.

When he was younger, before I can remember, before he was blind, Grandpa did things the way I do. Now, when we drink tea and eat lunch on the porch, Grandpa pours his own cup of tea by putting his finger just inside the rim of the cup to tell him when it is full. He never burns his finger. Afterward, when I wash the dishes, he feels them as he dries them. He even sends some back for me to wash again.

"Next time," says Grandpa, pretending to be cross, "I wash, you dry."

In the afternoon, Grandpa, Nana, and I take our books outside to read under the apple tree. Grandpa reads his book with his fingers, feeling the raised Braille dots that tell him the words.

As he reads, Grandpa laughs out loud.

"Tell us what's funny," says Nana. "Read to us, Papa."

And he does.

Nana and I put down our books to listen. A gray squirrel comes down the trunk of the apple tree, tail high, and seems to listen, too. But Grandpa doesn't see him.

After supper, Grandpa turns on the television. I watch, but Grandpa listens, and the music and the words tell him when something is dangerous or funny, happy or sad.

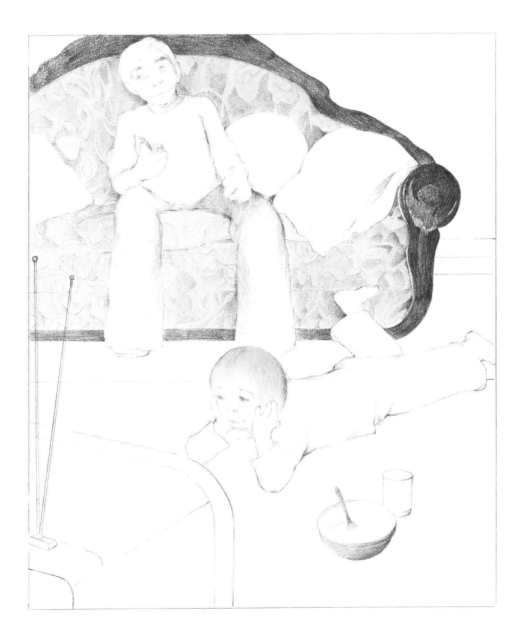

Somehow, Grandpa knows when it is dark, and he takes me upstairs and tucks me into bed. He bends down to kiss me, his hands feeling my head.

"You need a haircut, John," he says.

Before Grandpa leaves, he pulls the light chain above my bed to turn out the light. But, by mistake, he's turned it on instead. I lie for a moment after he's gone, smiling, before I get up to turn off the light.

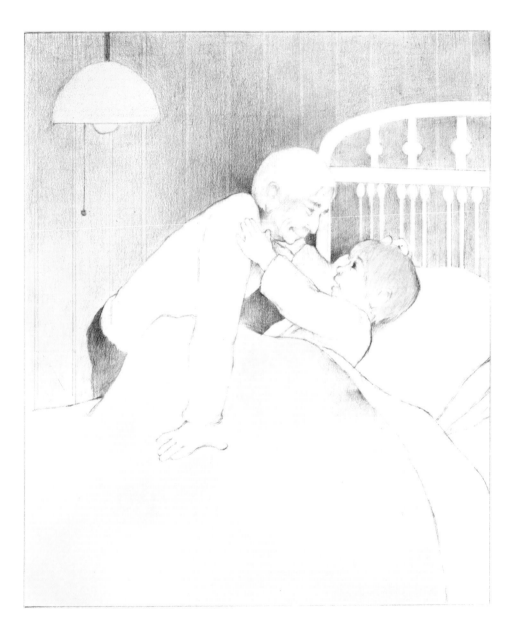

Then, when it is dark for me the way it is dark for Grandpa, I hear the night noises that Grandpa hears. The house creaking, the birds singing their last songs of the day, the wind rustling the tree outside my window.

Then, all of a sudden, I hear the sounds of geese overhead. They fly low over the house.

"Grandpa," I call softly, hoping he's heard them too.

"Honkers," he calls back.

"Go to sleep, John," says Nana.

Grandpa says her voice smiles to him. I test it.

"What?" I call to her.

"I said go to sleep," she answers.

She says it sternly. But Grandpa is right. Her voice smiles to me. I know. Because I'm looking through Grandpa's eyes.